AF480412

CHERRY

THE

BLACK
BERRY

PART 1

BY KRASI MIR

CHERRY THE BLACK BERRY
PART 1

Author: KRASI MIR
Editors: Sally Apokedak, Sarah Anderson de Ochoa
Illustrator: Tatsiana Tushyna

First edition 2024
ISBN 978-84-09-64158-1 (paperback)
ISBN 978-84-09-64028-7 (e-book)

Contents

Foreword

Cherry was born on Jun 4th, 2009, in Sofia, Bulgaria. She passed away peacefully on Apr 10th, 2023, in Barcelona, Spain with her best friends Krassy and Ani by her side. They had so much fun and laughter together, and they shared incredible stories. Cherry was a unique, exceptional, and irreplaceable friend.

She was really very special.

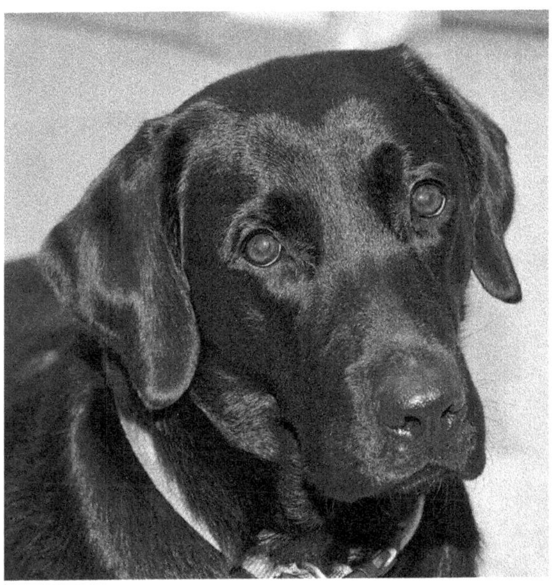

Dedication

To mom and dad, who planted the seeds of curiosity and knowledge and gave me the gift of dreams and courage to follow them. As a child, I was lucky to have access to a lot of books. My father and mother thoughtfully created a personal library in my room that became my reading haven. This was the greatest gift I could've hoped for. Captivated by the great stories, I spent countless hours reading and re-reading my favorites. Among these treasured tales were dog stories and thrilling adventures in the mountains, that fueled my interest to have a puppy one day and to explore the wilderness, eventually turning into a passionate reality and a beloved hobby.

To my son and his mother, you are the light of my life, my heart, living outside of me. Your laughter is my favorite music. You make my world complete.

To my brother, my blood and soul in a different body, I'm so proud and inspired by your journey and transformation to a healthier self, and I'm so happy for you.

To my grandparents, who now live in the stars—may this tale reach you. The amazing stories you told me, passed down by your ancestors, brought magic to my days and sparked my imagination.

To all who read these lines, thank you for giving my words a chance. May you feel the happiness contained within these pages.

To my dear dog Cherry—the main reason for writing and publishing this work. You'll be always with me in my memories, thoughts, and heart!

This book is dedicated to you all.

More splendid than gold in any land,
more dazzling than jewels so grand,
more beautiful than pearls in the sand,
more flawless than diamond rings,
more precious than all material things,
is the love of a dog and the joy it brings.

Cherry, a playful and smart black Lab,
is an endless source of fun and laughs.
With powerful energy and careless play,
she lights up the world in her own unique way.
But beware! She might steal your heart,
just like she did with mine from the start.

Learn about our adventures, happiness and delight
in the simple moments that make life so bright.
Feel the blessing of this companion merry,
I was so lucky to find in the Labrador Cherry.
This book is a humble tribute, heartfelt, and true,
to a dog so special like no other I ever knew…

The author

The Beginning

The ad jumped out at Krassy.

Newborn Labrador puppies to a loving home.

He'd always wanted a dog. A man's best friend. A constant companion in every season of life. It was his childhood dream. He wanted that more than anything.

His fingers trembled with anticipation as he dialed the number. When he hung up with an appointment set for Saturday, it felt unreal.

Am I really doing this?

He was ready to bring his dream to life.

Saturday morning, he made his way to the address the woman on the phone gave him.

Visions of long walks in the park and high in the mountains swam in his head.

A young woman, perhaps a few years older than himself, opened the door.

"You must be Krassy." She smiled warmly as she stepped forward.

"That's me, we spoke on the phone. I'm here to see the puppies." Krassy replied and held out his hand.

"I'm Ema. It's nice to meet you in person." She shook his hand. "Come on in—the puppies are in the backyard."

Krassy followed her through a garden filled with blooming roses and the soothing scent of lavender.

He spotted the puppies right away. They were jumping about, some of them engaged in wrestling matches with one another, and a few were entertained by their mother. A simple fence surrounded them, keeping them contained and preventing them from digging up the plants.

Krassy crouched down to get a closer look.

"They're so sweet! I don't know how I'm going to pick only one."

While he was just saying that one of the girl puppies cautiously approached Krassy and licked his hand. She was a bit smaller than the rest and had completely black fur.

She had a sweet and round face. Her big brown eyes were full of curiosity.

He scooped her up, bringing her closer so she could see him.

"Hi there." She licked his palm again.

"I think she is your puppy." Ema smiled, leaning against the enclosure.

"Looks like I don't have to choose anymore. She's chosen for me." Krassy's chest filled with warmth. "Cherry the Black Berry could be a good name." He thought about it for a second. "Or maybe Cherry, for short."

After tucking Cherry safely in a small box balanced on the back seat, Krassy drove home, being extra careful with every bump and turn.

He couldn't contain his disbelief he'd actually gotten a puppy.

He checked the rear-view mirror every few minutes. There she was, peaking up over the edge of the box. Her nose twitched with curiosity. It was her first time in a car.

Krassy pulled into the driveway and retrieved the box with Cherry inside. She was going to need a comfortable place to rest. He chose the quietest part of the living room and got the materials he'd purchased. A plastic dog bed with a soft pillow to put inside made a good home for the pup. Once he was finished, it was just right for a puppy to snuggle into.

After careful inspection, Cherry curled up at the back of the bed, her body shaking with anxiety. He'd read that young puppies could be overwhelmed by sudden separation from their mother and siblings.

"You'll settle in soon enough." He hoped that was the case. He wanted her to feel at home.

The next few days were hard. Cherry didn't want to leave her bed. She'd come out to eat and drink, then rush back inside.

Krassy kept a constant eye on her. What if something was wrong? He tried luring her out with toys, kind words, and treats. Nothing worked.

One afternoon, Cherry came out of bed for her food and water, but this time she didn't go directly back.

This time, she finally looked interested in her surroundings. She walked about the room, her nose twitching at every new smell and sight. Krassy watched as she explored all around her. Her tiny tail wagged back and forth.

She reminded him of a miniature toy.

Cherry moved from room to room. She found the kitchen intriguing and full of interesting smells.

She ventured into the cozy bedroom, stopping for a moment under the soft light streaming in from the window. When Cherry reached the balcony, she looked around—the world outside was vast and filled with unfamiliar sights and sounds.

Krassy imagined it had to be scary for such a small animal. Seeing the huge trees, the birds flying around, and the drop to the ground below. A gentle breeze floated by. It was all too much for Cherry.

She tucked her tail and dashed back to the living room and the safety of her bed.

Krassy followed and patted her head.

"Don't worry, Cherry. The world may seem now like a big and scary place to you, but we'll explore it together. One step at a time."

Cherry looked up at him and shook her head, as if to say, *"Maybe another time."*

Over the next three months, Cherry gained confidence. Although she spent most of her time indoors, she made a few curious trips to the balcony, always ending with a frantic sprint back inside.

She loved chasing flies and playing with the green tennis ball Krassy would toss and hide for her.

"Great catch, girl!" He cheered, watching her pounce on the ball. "Let me teach you to walk on a leash."

She was learning a lot about her new life. Soon enough, Cherry received her final vaccine. Now she could start exploring the outside world.

The real adventures were about to begin.

First Trip Outside

"Cherry!" Krassy called. She came running around the corner of the hallway and skidded to a halt at his feet with her tongue out. "It's time for your first trip outside!" She was four months old and fully vaccinated, so it was finally safe for an outdoor adventure. It was a long wait, but fully worth it.

The risk of Cherry getting sick from going out too early was enough to give Krassy the patience to wait.

He clipped the leash on her collar, and off they went. He'd picked the location for their first outing together—a waterfall up in the mountains not too far from his house.

He was relieved to see that they had a nice day to work with. It was sunny, and the sky was clear.

One day, he'd like Cherry to experience rain and even snow, but their first journey should be a nice experience.

Cherry wagged her tail with every step, as if to say, *"I'm ready to go places."* How she'd changed since he'd first brought her home.

"Look at you!" Krassy smiled as he watched her explore.

Cherry sniffed at every tree, rock, and patch of grass they passed along the forest path. He'd never seen her so excited. It seemed her bravery had grown a lot compared to her first days.

Krassy could imagine the different things she was smelling. Even he could smell the crisp pine needles and the sweet smell of wildflowers in the air.

The forest seemed alive. Birds chirped in the branches around, and another dog barked far away. A small creature darted off their path before they could clearly see what it was.

Cherry spotted a bird sitting on a low branch.

She reached forward and barked playfully. The bird was not happy with this. It let out a frightened squawk and flapped its wings as it flew off.

"Nice try, Cherry." Krassy laughed. "I'll have to teach you to leave the other animals alone. Now, let's move on! We have a waterfall to see," he pulled her back to the path.

Krassy enjoyed this trail every time he walked it. The path led through the forest, with a green canopy overhead. The leaves of the trees let little spots of sunlight through, making bright patterns on the ground.

Cherry darted back and forth, leading the way. A patch of wildflowers in purple, yellow, and pink colors caught her attention.

She stuck her nose deep in the blossoms, sneezing loudly. Krassy shook his head.

"Bless you!" He gave her a gentle pat on the neck.

It was almost an hour before they arrived at the waterfall. Krassy drew in a sharp breath at the sight.

Water crashed down the rocks in a thunderous roar. It shimmered in the sunlight, creating a faint rainbow in the mist. Droplets of water covered him and Cherry like a refreshing blanket.

"Here we go, Cherry," Krassy said, putting down his backpack. "A break and a snack sound perfect about now, what do you think?"

They sat on the bank of the small lake at the waterfall's base. Krassy unpacked a sandwich for himself and gave a few treats to Cherry. While he ate, Cherry explored the lake's edge, sniffing at the smooth pebbles and lapping up the cool, crystal-clear water.

Without any warning, she launched herself into the water. Krassy looked with tension until he saw her paddling around happily.

He watched her first swim with a smile and pride blooming in his chest.

Labradors are known for their love of water, and he was glad that Cherry was no exception.

Her black fur sparkled as she came back to shore, shaking off the water in a glittering shower of droplets.

"You liked your first swim, Cherry, didn't you!" Krassy smiled, handing her another treat.

After their break, it was time to head back home. The trail was full of rocks, fallen branches, and occasional inclines.

As they walked, Cherry's pace slowed. The thrill of the day was too much for her.

"Getting tired, little one?" Krassy asked as Cherry trailed behind. It seemed as if she'd lost all of her usual energy.

Cherry tilted her head to the side with a look that said, *"It was a long walk for me."* Her steps were somewhat sluggish and weary. She was so tiny that Krassy easily took her into his arms. It wasn't surprising she was exhausted after everything they'd done today—Cherry was still a puppy.

She nuzzled into him and licked his hand as if to say, *"Thank you!"*

"I've got you," Krassy stroked gently her head before continuing his walk.

Cherry's eyes grew heavy as he carried her down the trail. The steady rhythm of his footsteps and the warmth of his hug seemed so soothing to her.

Soon, she fell asleep, her body getting heavier in his arms.

Krassy didn't mind the peaceful walk back. He had the forest to keep him company. Cherry's chest rose and fell with each breath. She was so calm and content in his arms.

The sun was setting down, painting the sky in oranges and yellows when they got back home.

Cherry stirred and opened her eyes as Krassy put her gently into her bed.

He sat next to her and scratched her behind the ears, thinking about their day.

"If you enjoyed today, you're going to love all the adventures I've planned," Krassy whispered. "Good night now, have some sleep."

Cherry wagged her tail as if she understood. Then she turned over and slept peacefully throughout the night.

Training class

It was early Sunday morning, and Krassy was still in bed. He felt a gentle lick on his palm in his sleep. He stirred and opened his eyes to see Cherry standing next to his bed, panting, and giving the illusion of a smile on her face. She licked his fingers again, her warm eyes urging him to start the day.

"Good morning, Cherry," Krassy said, sleepily stretching his arms and letting out a big yawn. Cherry's tail thumped against the bed frame several times as if it were a morning trumpet playing a cheerful *get-up* tune. She waited patiently for him to get out of bed and get dressed, watching his every move.

Krassy headed down the hall to the kitchen, with Cherry following him closely.

"I have something pretty exciting planned today," he said with a smile.

"You are going to have your first doggy training class after breakfast."

Cherry wagged her tail even more, her ears perking up at the word *breakfast*. She didn't understand what he was saying about dog school yet, but soon she would.

After preparing himself a bowl of oatmeal, yogurt, and berries, he dished up Cherry's favorite dog chow, and the two ate together, Cherry down on the floor and him at the dining room table.

Once they were done eating, Krassy got ready with his running shoes and grabbed Cherry's leash from the hook by the door. She nearly knocked him over with her eagerness to go outside. She had already learned what the leash meant.

It didn't take long to get to the park. Cherry was pulling him ahead, so Krassy almost ran after her. The sun beat down on them, heating the sidewalk. They kept going further into the park, keeping an eye out for the training class.

It was easy to spot—a large and open space crowded with dogs of every breed and their owners, trying their best to keep all the dogs in a circle.

The trainer, a tall, skinny man in a red shirt, was smiling cheerfully.

"Good morning, all! Now that most of you are here, we'll start the class. Today, we'll focus on the *sit* command. Let's start by walking in a circle with our dogs."

Krassy joined the group, Cherry bouncing alongside, her tail a blur of motion. So many friends for her to get to know!

Krassy pulled her along with him as they walked around in a wide circle. He paid attention to what the trainer did, lifting his hand with a treat.

At the trainer's signal, they all stopped and repeated the command, "Sit."

Instead of sitting, Cherry pulled forward, nipping at the dog in front of her, throwing herself into a playful tussle.

Krassy pulled back on her leash.

"Get back here, Cherry." She was very bad at listening. Not too surprising, considering how much raw energy a Labrador had.

"Let's do it again." The trainer kept the pace beside them. When he stopped for the sit command, Cherry darted to the back, straight toward the dog behind them. Krassy shook his head, putting on his most patient smile.

"Alright, Cherry," he said, placing her on a short leash so she couldn't get to the other dogs. Cherry wasn't pleased. She barked in a high-pitched tone, as if complaining. The other dogs answered with a chorus of barks, like they were trying to comfort her.

"Cherry, quiet down." Krassy tried to calm her, but she wouldn't listen. The barking had everyone distracted and made it impossible for the trainer to communicate anything to the rest of the group.

"Here, how about I take the leash this time?" he offered. Just as the trainer was wrapping his fingers around the leash, Cherry took off. The leash slipped through his fingers, and she was off, a black streak through the green field. She darted forward, running across the park.

Some of the other dogs followed her example, pulling from their owner's grasp and racing after her.

She led them around the park, zigzagging between the trees and bushes. The rest of the dogs didn't seem to mind the unexpected interruption to their class one bit. They barked loudly and continued with their chase.

After a while, Cherry got a little tired.

She stopped at a nearby stream and looked behind, as if to say, *"Now, watch this!"* Without any hesitation, she jumped right in for a refreshing swim.

The rest of the pack followed her example, plunging into the clear water with sheer excitement.

Krassy and the dog owners ran after them, laughing and shouting, trying to catch up.

"Cherry, come back here!" Krassy called, chuckling as he jogged.

"Look at them go!" Another owner laughed. "It's like a dog parade!"

Eventually, they reached the creek, where all the dogs were having the time of their lives, playing in the cold water.

"Oh my gosh, they're soaked!" somebody exclaimed, wading into the stream.

"Fun's over!" A tall man said as he was pulling a sopping-wet husky from the water.

Each owner managed to retrieve their pet from the stream. Cherry was the last. Krassy couldn't bring himself to be upset when he saw the delight in her eyes.

Her fluffy, black fur was plastered, making her look strange. He laughed at the sight.

"I should've known you'd take off. You'd do anything to get near water." Krassy said.

Another one of the dog owners was patting a poodle down with a towel.

"They're unpredictable, aren't they?" she asked. "My dog doesn't usually like the water, but it seems she was pulled along by peer pressure."

Krassy nodded with another chuckle.

"Cherry is unstoppable when it comes to water. She managed to derail the entire class." He shook his head. He'd hoped to make an impression, but he thought it would be a different one than having the dog that distracted everyone else.

The owners had all gathered by the stream. Some dried their dogs, and others waited for them to drip dry. The atmosphere was energetic, despite the unexpected interruption to the class.

"That was exciting!" one owner said with a laugh in Krassy's direction.

"We haven't had so much fun in a while."

"Cherry really knows how to liven things up," another added, patting Cherry on the back as she passed.

The trainer approached Krassy.

"I think that's enough excitement for one day. We had a great laugh and a good run, thanks to you and Cherry."

"I meant to warn you when I passed you the leash. She has a mind of her own for sure and a lot of energy," Krassy said, trying to craft an apology.

The trainer waved it off. "This was one of the most entertaining classes we've had this year, so don't worry about it. Everyone enjoyed it, including the dogs. We'll continue next time."

He turned to Krassy. "You can start working with Cherry on commands at home.

When you say "*Sit*", gently guide her into a sitting position and she'll understand. Remember to give her small treats to keep her focused and reward her when she follows the command."

Krassy nodded, grateful for the suggestion. "I'll definitely try that."

The trainer clapped him on the shoulder.

"Labradors are highly trainable dogs. They learn quickly with consistency, patience, and small rewards. They're very playful, as we all saw today, so they learn best when they're having fun."

"Cherry and I have some fun time every day. I'll certainly add training elements to our to-do list." Krassy replied.

"Start with the basic commands, like sit, stay, come." The trainer shook Krassy's hand. "When she learns these, continue with more advanced tricks. Cherry is a great dog, and like I said, Labradors are perfect for training. High-energy dogs can be a challenge at first, but they are also the most rewarding."

"I can't wait to get started, and I suppose I'll have to make sure there's no water for her to get into," Krassy joked. "Thanks for the advice, and thanks everyone for the good time," he added, waving goodbye to the trainer and the group.

Cherry trotted beside him, water still dripping from her wet, glistening fur, her tongue hanging out.

"Ready for some more training, Cherry?" Krassy asked as they reached home. Cherry barked, her eyes bright with excitement.

"Let's see if we can master that *sit* command without running around an entire park twice, huh?" Krassy laughed, unlocking the door. With a final pat on Cherry's neck, they stepped inside, content after the playful lesson and the eventful day.

Pizza Slice in the Bushes

Krassy and Cherry fell into a routine as the days passed. One afternoon, they went for a walk near their home. Cherry, an ever-crazy package of energy, led the way, her nose to the ground.

As they turned the corner at the end of the road, Cherry jumped on her leash, pulling toward some bushes.

"What is it, Cherry?" Krassy peered at the bushes, looking for anything out of the ordinary.

She kept going forward, then dove into the leaves. A second later, her head popped up, a piece of pizza in her mouth. Someone must have accidentally dropped it.

Cherry's eyes twinkled with excitement, the slice dangling from her mouth, full of slobber and a bit of dirt.

"Cherry, you can't eat that! Who knows how long it's been there?" Krassy reached for the pizza but was too late.

The pizza was gone in one fell swoop, straight down Cherry's throat. She licked her lips and pranced about as if nothing happened.

Krassy shook his head, standing there, unease settling over him. Would it make her sick? What if there was something dangerous on that pizza? There was nothing he could do but keep an eye on her.

Thankfully, there was no sign of anything being wrong, and it continued that way.

After the pizza incident, every walk near the house turned into a trip to the bushes where Cherry found the pizza. No matter how many turns or what route they tried, Cherry always pulled Krassy back to the same bush to search for a tasty treasure. Krassy was nothing but impressed by her determination.

"Back to the pizza bush again, huh, Cherry?" Krassy would ask while following her lead.

Another afternoon, after a walk and an unsuccessful visit to the infamous pizza bush, they passed an elderly woman's house. She was their neighbor in the sense that she lived on the same block. A small box of cat food sat on the pavement outside, most likely to feed the street cats.

Cherry didn't hesitate. She lunged toward the box and gobbled up a mouthful of food.

"Cherry, no! That's for the cats!" Krassy pulled her away from the box.

Cherry looked up with an innocent expression while licking her lips.

From then on, whenever they passed the elderly woman's house, Cherry would try to sneak some cat food.

Krassy soon realized what she was after and tried to change their route to avoid the house and the pizza bush,

but Cherry's nose and determination took them back to those familiar spots time and time again.

"You're a stubborn one, aren't you?" Krassy laughed as Cherry veered back to her preferred route, which included the snacking stops.

When Krassy got home, he looked it up. He was curious to find out more about Cherry's peculiar habits.

"Did you know you have three hundred million receptors in your nose?" he asked her, giving Cherry a curious look as he scrolled through an article. He was surprised to find that humans only had around six million, and that meant Cherry's sense of smell was between ten and one hundred times more sensitive than his.

Cherry tipped her head at the information and watched him intently, as if she was eager to hear more.

"Here's one for you," he continued. "Your sense of smell is so precise that you can distinguish hot from cold water by scent alone."

He read on to find out that Labradors could also smell small chemical substances, called pheromones, which other animals, even insects, and especially mammals release through their bodies.

"Imagine that," he mumbled. He didn't realize Labradors had superpowers. It made sense, since the smelling pheromones made them excellent at tracking and recognizing emotions.

"I found out why you're always sniffing," Krassy informed a still-interested Cherry.

"You have a separate airway for sniffing, and it doesn't disrupt your breathing. You really are something." As he continued to read, he chuckled to himself.

There was a section on how Labradors could distinguish between layers of smell. Like recognizing individual ingredients in a stew or different scents in crowded spaces. That would be a pretty nifty skill for a chef if dogs were allowed to cook.

The cat food scenario made a lot of sense when Krassy read the distance Labradors could smell a scent from. Up to one mile or more than one and a half kilometers away in ideal conditions. He started to wonder if their trip to the old lady's house with the cat food was ever an accident.

The most endearing fact he learned about Cherry that day was that she had very good memory.

Her exceptional memory was most responsible for her returning to the spots where she found treats. It was also the reason Labradors excelled at search and rescue tasks or identifying some diseases.

But it also meant that no matter what happened, she'd always remember him, and that was something truly special.

The Picnic

It was a bright and early morning when Krassy decided they were going to do something different for the day. Cherry was making her normal rounds about the house, full of endless energy.

"Cherry," he called her over. "Do you want to go to a picnic?"

Her feet tapped on the floor, making little clicking sounds when the hard nails touched the tiles. *"Of course I do."* Her tail wagged with enthusiasm as if saying, *"Let's go."* A picnic meant food and funny games.

Krassy filled a basket with delicious sandwiches, fresh fruit, and a full bag of dog treats for Cherry. The walk to the park was a quick one, it was rather a run, actually.

Cherry didn't hold back.

She practically dragged Krassy toward the park. She knew the place well and only stopped momentarily to greet passing dogs. At the park, they searched around for a great picnic spot. Right in the middle of the park was Krassy's favorite place.

A huge oak tree sat in the center of the field. Its branches spread wide, covering a large section of the grass below with shade. It was the perfect cool spot for a hot summer day. Krassy spread out a checkered quilt underneath it. It was the designated picnic blanket. After all, it wouldn't be a picnic without a blanket to enjoy lunch on. Cherry plopped down on top of it as soon as it hit the ground.

Krassy started unloading the basket, and Cherry watched with unwavering attention. There were ham and cheese sandwiches, juicy apples, and a special treat—a bone-shaped cookie just for her. He liked bringing something different for her on picnics. It set the event apart from their normal outings and daily routines.

"Now, Cherry, don't eat this all at once, try to make it last," Krassy said with a wink.

He got comfortable against the trunk of the tree with a sandwich and an apple in hand. Cherry enjoyed some treats and extras from the basket before deciding to explore the park. She started out nearby, and little by little, she moved further away.

Something caught her attention.

A couple of kids were kicking a ball around not too far away. Cherry dove into their game, grabbing at the ball.

At first, the children protested before they started laughing and chased her. The game was on. Whenever they'd kick the ball in Cherry's direction, she'd stop it and push it around with her nose before they got it back.

Immersed in her ball game, it looked like she belonged to the kids. She stopped suddenly, and her ears perked up. Cherry turned in the direction of the sound. Her eyes locked in on a brown squirrel on the ground, near one of the trees around.

The little critter darted up the tree trunk, its bushy tail flicking as it climbed higher.

Cherry dropped the ball and forgot all about the game with the kids. She took off after the squirrel, barking up the tree as if to say, *"Come down here and play!"*

Krassy sighed, knowing that Cherry's fascination with squirrels was an endless source of entertainment and sometimes trouble. He went over to where Cherry was making a fuss, the grass cool beneath his feet.

"Cherry, leave the poor squirrel alone," he said, tugging gently on her leash. He'd left it on in case he had to catch up to her and restrain her.

Cherry looked back longingly at the squirrel as Krassy pulled her away.

He knew it was a lot of fun for her, but not so much for the smaller animals she wanted to terrorize.

Her ears perked up again, and she tilted her head, locking in on some movement across the park.

A German shepherd was walking down the sidewalk, its owner by its side. It was black, just like Cherry. She seemed to make the same connection, because the next thing he knew, she was off, galloping across the park with her leash trailing behind her.

Krassy chased after her, and shortly after, he managed to reach the spot where she was sniffing the other dog nose to nose.

"Sorry about her. Cherry loves other dogs," Krassy managed to wheeze out.

"That's okay. Charlie always enjoys another friend." The dog's owner laughed and put out his hand. "I'm Tony, by the way."

"Nice to meet you. I'm Krassy," he said while trying to get his breathing under control.

Tony unclipped Charlie.

"How about we give them a minute to play?"

Krassy nodded, and they watched the two dogs take off together with a leap.

They chased each other in circles, played tug-of-war with a stick, and even tried to dig a hole together, their paws kicking up the soft earth.

Krassy and Tony watched on with amusement.

They fell into an easy conversation about the dogs and swapped a few embarrassing and funny stories. There were some experiences that appeared to be common for pet owners.

As the afternoon stretched on, Cherry wore herself out. Tony and his dog said goodbye and left.

Krassy and Cherry retreated to their picnic blanket to pack up their stuff before heading back home.

The sun colored the clouds in orange tones as it started to set. The air became cooler.

Cherry, now exhausted from her day of fun, was already dreaming of a nap. On the way back, she laid down in the middle of the sidewalk and simply refused to move further.

"Cherry, what are you doing? You can't sleep on the sidewalk." Krassy gave the leash a firm tug, but it was useless.

He tried a treat and picked her up so she was in a walking position. Nothing worked. "Are you going to make me carry you now?"

She lifted her head and tilted it to the side, as if to say, *"Pretty please."*

"Fine," Krassy grumbled, scooping her up against his shoulder. He was going to have to carry her home. The people they passed looked amused.

"You sure are a spoiled pup," Krassy teased, while Cherry licked his face happily.

Back at home, Krassy prepared dinner, and Cherry wolfed everything down.

They both fell onto the couch after dinner, ready for a moment of relaxation. Cherry's eyes grew heavy, and soon she was snoring, her head resting on Krassy's lap.

Krassy stroked Cherry's shiny black fur and smiled, thinking about the day's adventures.

"You sure know how to keep life interesting, Cherry," he whispered.

Cherry's tail wagged in her sleep, as if she understood him.

Krassy knew that, with Cherry by his side, every day would be full of laughter and joy.

At the Beach

Krassy sang along with the music on the radio. They were halfway to the beach—what he considered a proper road trip for him and Cherry. He'd been planning it for quite some time. Since Cherry loved the water so much, the beach seemed like the perfect idea for her.

He glanced back at Cherry. Her head was hanging out the window, her tongue flapping in the wind. He always wondered how it was that her mouth didn't dry out doing that. He chuckled.

He'd made sure to pack everything they would need that morning for a great day on the beach.

As they left the city behind, the landscape changed. Flat green fields stretched out on either side, with the occasional trees here and there.

Cherry barked at every car that passed.

At last, Krassy got his first look at the beach. Whenever he could, he would spare a glance from the road, taking in the vast blue body of water.

Getting to the beach was somewhat of a long drive, and when Krassy pulled into the beach parking, he was itching to get out and stretch his legs.

"Are you ready, Cherry? I think you're going to love this." He got her leash ready and stood poised by the door to get her out. Cherry wasn't very good at listening, and it was always a struggle when they went to places. For the most part, she never got into too much trouble before Krassy could stop her.

She was ready, her whole body tense, and waiting for him to open the door. He prepared the leash, intending to snap it onto her collar as soon as she was still. Cherry had other plans. She took off running at full speed, almost knocking Krassy down as she raced toward the water. Endless water, as far as she could see. It was a dream come true for Cherry.

Krassy had picked this beach for a reason—it didn't require dogs to be on a leash, and that meant he could take his time. He made his way down to the sand in pursuit of Cherry. Once he got to the shore, he took his time setting up his towel and sunshade. A blur of black fur off to the right caught his attention.

Cherry was coming back from the water, soaking wet and dripping with salt. She skidded to a halt right in front of him, wagging her tail as if to thank him for bringing her along.

"I knew you'd love it, girl." He pulled one of her favorite treats from the beach bag and tossed it to her.

She caught it mid-air with a snap. Reaching into the bag again, he drew out something else that she loved just as much, if not more than a treat.

"Do you want to play?" He shook a green tennis ball back and forth, and Cherry's whole head followed its every movement. "All right then, go fetch!"

Cherry took off without being asked again. He was amazed by how she was able to track the ball through the sand, no matter how far he threw it.

Cherry was such an energetic dog; every game he came up with, she was happy to play.

After a while of playing catch, his arm was a bit sore, so he tucked the ball away in the bag and headed down the beach.

Excited for some exploring, Cherry took off ahead. She veered off his path and ran up the beach a ways, stopping where some kids were building a sandcastle. The kids were clearly expert builders. Their castle had little windows carved into it, seashells for doors, and a huge moat just in case the waves were to make it that far up the beach.

Cherry seemed as impressed as he was. She rooted around with her nose, pushing at the sides of the castle. Krassy picked up the pace. She was about to destroy some innocent kids' castle.

"Cherry, wait!" He ran as fast as he could to stop her. By the time he arrived, the castle was completely destroyed.

He expected tears. Instead, the kids were fascinated with Cherry. They took turns petting her, and they didn't seem too upset about their castle at all. Krassy felt guilty; he'd seen how hard they worked on the castle.

"Would you guys like some help rebuilding this?" Krassy offered.

"Yes! Can she help too?" one of the kids asked.

"Cherry would love to help. She's a great digger." Krassy reassured them.

Cherry went wild, digging so fast in the sand which she sent flying in every direction as if to prove his point. The kids burst into laughter.

Between all of them, they built a mansion of a sandcastle that was two times bigger than the previous.

By the time they were done, Krassy had new respect for the kids. Sandcastles were a lot more work than they looked like.

Krassy and Cherry said goodbye to the children and headed back to the sea.

The sun was low, making it the perfect time for a swim without getting burned. Well, at least Cherry didn't have to worry about that. Krassy realized that something like sun lotion would be useless for her. The two of them swam in the sea, ducking under waves, and searched for shells in the sand for the next couple of hours.

Krassy loved the warm air. It made the water feel refreshing instead of cold. A spray of water hit him every time a wave crashed down.

Sometimes Cherry would face the waves head-on, trying to catch them in her mouth. Krassy laughed at her antics, wishing he had his camera with him.

After they were thoroughly exhausted, they headed back to the towel for a snack.

Krassy had some of his favorite sandwiches and Cherry—a few of her tastiest treats to enjoy. They watched the sunset as they finished eating, then Krassy packed up everything he'd brought.

It wasn't a short way to travel for a day of fun, but he thought every minute was worth it. After all, it was time well spent with a friend who meant a lot to him.

"What did you think, Cherry? Do you love the beach as much as I do?" He was almost positive that she nodded in her unique doggy way.

Happy with the day well spent, they got back in the car and started their drive home. Every day with Cherry was an adventure, and Krassy had a feeling they would continue to have many more.

Tom and Cherry

An evening walk became a routine thing for Krassy and Cherry. It was always nice to spend some time outside. Raining, snowing, or a bit windy – it didn't matter much. Walking on the street, enjoying the peaceful neighborhood, and taking some fresh air was a favorite for Krassy and Cherry. Sometimes they would take known paths, and other times they'd try to find a new place to explore.

Cherry loved the outdoors. She enjoyed the new smells—the scent of cut grass or the earthy aroma after it rained.

There was a house on their normal route. It was almost right next door to theirs. There was a cat that lived there named Tom. He was a beautiful cat. Even Krassy could see that, despite being more of a dog person.

The way the cat carried himself made it clear he considered himself king of the neighborhood.

Avoiding Tom's house wasn't an option. Whenever they would pass, Tom would tease Cherry.

He would walk back and forth, right in front of her, but far enough out of her reach that he was in no danger of being caught.

Cherry enjoyed these interactions with Tom. Either she didn't realize that the cat was trying to make fun of her or she didn't care, Krassy was never sure. She would put her nose through the gaps of the white fence that separated Tom's yard from the street, trying to get a sniff of him.

Tom liked to tease Cherry further. He'd smack her nose with his paw, and she'd jerk back, a bewildered look on her face. Most likely, this was his way of telling her to stay away.

It would only work Cherry up even more. It was amusing to watch Tom swiping from one side and Cherry watching his movements from the other side of the fence.

During their usual walk one evening, Tom was in front of the fence. He was stretched out, enjoying the late sunlight when Krassy and Cherry walked by. Cherry yanked on her leash, leaping forward with everything she had. Krassy wasn't prepared for her efforts, and Cherry got her way.

Tom darted back to safety behind the fence. Cherry sniffed through the gaps, while Tom swiped at her from his side.

"Easy, girl!" Krassy chuckled, trying to keep up. This game became a common occurrence. Tom would sneak in and out of the fence on occasion, adding an element of surprise.

As the crickets began their nightly serenade, Cherry and Krassy were once more on their walk when they spotted Tom outside the fence again.

Cherry was ready this time. She rushed forward with such force that her leash snapped.

Krassy's heart sank. He was worried Cherry would actually catch the cat after all.

"Cherry, don't!" Krassy tried to stop her, but he was too slow, or maybe she was too quick.

Cherry was already in full pursuit. She was focused on Tom, determined to get him for once.

Tom ran hard, as quickly as his legs allowed. He made sharp turns and twists in an attempt to lose his follower, but he couldn't. Cherry was right behind him, not letting up a single bit. They ran, zigzagging across the lawn.

Tom dove to the left and climbed up the fence, only stopping when he was at the top.

Cherry skidded to a halt below, her tongue hanging out as she barked up at Tom as if asking him to come down and play some more.

Krassy eventually caught up, panting and out of breath. He grabbed Cherry and secured her with what was left of the leash.

Tom, meanwhile, looked down at them from his perch, his tail waving back and forth with pride.

"I think we need a stronger leash," Krassy said, chuckling.

Tom and Cherry continued with their games whenever there was an opportunity.

Krassy got a thicker and wider harness, but this didn't stop Cherry from sneaking out by pulling so hard and unexpectedly the leash that it would slip from Krassy's hands.

The cat and dog show provided never-ending entertainment for the neighbors, who often stopped to watch the amusing games of this unusual pair.

One day, Cherry and Krassy passed by while Tom was on top of the fence with a toy mouse in his paws.

Cherry's eyes lit up with excitement. When they got near enough, Tom dropped the toy mouse in an almost intentional way.

Cherry let out a bark of joy as she grabbed it and gave it a vigorous shake.

"Well, well, Tom is sharing today." Krassy watched on with a laugh.

From that moment forward, it seemed as if a connection was made between the two fury friends.

Little things started to appear by the sidewalk, right where Krassy and Cherry would walk by.

Sometimes a small ball, other times—different toys. It was as if Tom left these gifts for Cherry.

Cherry always looked for the surprises, and sometimes she would try to push the toys back through the fence gaps as if returning them to Tom.

Krassy watched with a smile at how their bond grew stronger—he enjoyed the sight of the two friends interacting. What Tom and Cherry had was something special, a reminder that friendship knows no boundaries and can blossom in the most unexpected ways.

Flying Disk Chase

At the park, Krassy showed the special surprise he'd bought for Cherry the last time he went to the dog store. It was a large, round flying disk in bright red, so it wouldn't get lost easily. When he saw it there on the shelf, he instantly knew she'd enjoy it.

Krassy would often get new dog toys or different treats for his furry friend. Even the most durable items couldn't last for too long, so they had to be replaced from time to time. And Cherry was like a small child enjoying these new toys. It was fun to watch and to play with.

"Want to give it a try?" He'd seen many videos of dogs catching disks in midair. It seemed like a fun game, especially for Retrievers, who love to chase pretty much everything that moves.

Cherry's eyes flashed with excitement.

"Here you go!" He sent the disk flying through the air. Cherry took off below it, looking up to keep track of it. Krassy heard the click of her jaw as she chomped down on the disk.

She grabbed it, holding it in her mouth till she came back to the ground. No one would have guessed it was her first time playing with a disk.

He imagined what it would look like in slow motion. Krassy chuckled at the mental image.

It was most likely going to rain that evening, judging by the clouds in the sky. They blocked the sun, so it wasn't too hot while running around.

Summer was a great time to be in the park. It was full of flowers, and the sweet smell they filled the air with. The grass was a dark green, showing just how much water it had—enough to be at its best.

Krassy threw the disk again. This time, he sent it up higher. Cherry was just about to catch it when a Golden Retriever came out of nowhere. The other dog was bigger and bulkier. He intercepted the flying round object, snatching the disk in his mouth. He took off, leaving both Krassy and Cherry in the dust as he headed across the park.

Krassy ran after the dog, with Cherry not too far behind him.

The Retriever dashed between trees, zigzagged across paths, and finally, in a bold move, jumped into the park's small lake. Cherry followed right in. Krassy wasn't sure if Cherry was still trying to get the disk back or if she was just distracted by the water.

He circled around to the other side of the lake, intending to stop the retriever when he got out of the water.

The dog changed direction halfway across the lake, then leaped out on the opposite side before Krassy could reach him.

He was a crafty opponent and very quick.

Cherry stepped out of the water, droplets sliding down her fur, shaking herself off and continuing the chase.

Krassy followed.

The dog kept rushing through the park with the disk tightly in his mouth, clearly enjoying this game. It seemed like he had no plans of stopping.

Krassy had to admit that it looked fun. If he was a dog, it was probably exactly what he'd be doing.

Cherry and Krassy, though tired, didn't give up. They forced themselves to keep running, breathing in short bursts.

Just when it seemed like they would never catch the dog, he dropped the disk without warning, heading off in the direction that he'd come from.

The animal vanished into the park as quickly as he had emerged. One moment he was there, leading Cherry and Krassy on a wild pursuit, and the next moment he disappeared behind the trees and bushes.

The Golden Retriever and the chase for the disk were unexpected surprises. The swim in the pond was great too, and it certainly added an interesting element to the day. Krassy, still recovering his breath, looked down at Cherry.

"That was so funny!" he gasped. "At least we got our disk back."

Cherry wagged her tail in agreement, and Krassy patted her neck.

An older gentleman sat on a nearby park bench. He was close enough to have seen the whole thing. Krassy looked over to find the man clutching his sides with laughter.

"The two of you put on quite the show. I've read that a dog can extend your life by about ten years just from all the exercise you get."

"I believe it," Krassy agreed. He smiled at the thought.

"The two of you made that run look like it was nothing, crossing the park so fast."

The old man shook his head. "I remember when I could run like that. Never take it for granted."

Krassy tried to picture it—him and Cherry chasing after a random Golden Retriever with a bright red disk in its mouth.

"Take care!" Krassy waved goodbye to the old man, leaving him behind on the bench. He wondered what brought him to the park. Whatever the reason, it was great to see how Cherry cheered him up a bit.

Krassy smiled as he spotted the coveted disk in Cherry's mouth. The unexpected twist in their adventure added even more fun to their trip. Krassy walked home with Cherry by his side and a happy feeling in his chest.

The sun set as they reached the house, bringing an end to another great day. Krassy was sure there were many more to come.

Fire Alarm

Krassy gave the last piece of toast a flip. He was almost done toasting bread for dinner to go along with the salad. It all smelled delicious, making his stomach growl.

Cherry seemed to have the same idea because she was rolling around on the floor, looking up at him expectantly for any scraps he'd be willing to send her way.

It was the usual sight when Krassy was cooking something in the kitchen. He would never throw away any food if it was safe for Cherry to eat it. So, she made sure she sticks around Krassy, and she was always rewarded.

The neighbors' kids were releasing sky lanterns outside. Their laughter echoed through the twilight.

It was a beautiful sight to see the paper balloons, with their glowing candles, drifting gracefully into the dusk sky, flashing like small stars.

The gentle breeze carried the lanterns further and further away until they became small blinking dots in the distance. The kids, excited by this interesting activity, kept launching more and more lanterns. They giggled loudly and clapped their hands after each successful release.

Cherry padded across the floor, retreating to her bed. She rested her snout on her paws, and then suddenly she lifted her head back up and smelled the air.

A curious scent tickled her nostrils.

It wasn't the usual scent of grilled bread or fresh vegetables. No, this was different.

It was smoke.

Cherry sat up, her nose twitching madly. She barked once, then twice, trying to get Krassy's attention.

Krassy was busy in the kitchen and didn't notice at first. He hummed along with a tune playing on the radio as he put his finished bread into a basket and covered it with a towel.

Cherry barked louder. She ran to the kitchen, her claws clicking as she went. She latched onto Krassy's pants, tugging at them.

"What is it, Cherry?" Her behavior was strange. Usually, she would wait patiently for dinner.

She barked again and once more grabbed onto his pants, pulling him toward the front of the house.

"Cherry, I have to finish dinner. I can't take you outside right now." He had already turned off the grill, so he humored, going out to the porch.

They walked down the steps, and that was when he stopped and looked up. Krassy drew in a sharp breath. A thin trail of smoke rose from the top of the porch roof.

One of the paper balloons was trapped, and the dry wood was beginning to catch fire.

The wind must have pushed the sky lantern towards Krassy's house, and somehow it ended up under the porch wooden ceiling. Meanwhile, the kids were too busy releasing more and more lanterns, so nobody really noticed that one of them got trapped.

"Oh no!" Krassy shouted, his heart racing. He thought of calling the fire department, but what if the fire spread further while he was looking for his phone? In his distress, he couldn't even remember where he had left it.

He grabbed a nearby garden hose and rapidly sprayed the area, putting out the flames. He exhaled with relief and turned to Cherry. "Good girl, Cherry! Well done!"

But this wasn't all. Cherry started barking again, this time tugging Krassy back into the kitchen.

He had turned off the grill, but a few pieces of bread were still on top of it, and they caught fire.

Flames licked the cabinets above. His heart pounded as he worked to put it out.

"Goodness, what's happening with all these fires?"

Krassy quickly grabbed a glass from the top of the kitchen counter and filled it with water from the faucet. He sprayed the bread and the flames as much as he could. This helped a little, but it seemed that more water was needed. He poured a second glass and this time it was enough. Krassy immediately opened the window, so the smoke could easily escape.

Once the flames were out, the kitchen was a disaster. He'd managed to get water everywhere, and his dinner was a soggy mess. Krassy leaned against the counter, drawing in a few calming breaths.

Cherry sat not too far off, her tail wagging, but her eyes were full of anxiety, as if wondering if he was all right. She had saved the day, not once, but twice.

"You're my hero, Cherry," Krassy said, hugging her hard. Cherry licked his face, pleased to have helped.

Krassy couldn't stop thinking about how close they had come to tragedy tonight. If Cherry hadn't alerted him to the first fire and then the second, who knows what could have happened.

The entire home might have burned down. He gave Cherry a treat and rubbed behind her ears. "You deserve it, girl. You saved both of us tonight." Cherry woofed softly, as if acknowledging his words.

The evening had taken an unexpected turn, but thanks to Cherry, everything turned out okay.

Later, as Krassy sat down to enjoy the salad with fewer slices of toasted bread, he looked at Cherry with admiration.

"You're more than just a dog, Cherry. You're my guardian angel." Cherry wagged her tail and settled down next to Krassy. She might not understand all the words, but she knew she had done something good.

And for a dog, that was the best feeling in the world.

Countryside Trip

"Cherry, how about we take a trip to the countryside today?" Krassy asked one sleepy Sunday morning.

Cherry stopped stretching and yawning. Her ears perked up at the word *trip*, and her tail wagged with enthusiasm like a windmill, spinning in a summer breeze. They had been to lots of places but had only gone to the countryside once before. Little by little, the opportunities to go with a dog to many different places presented themselves.

Once Krassy had everything loaded up into the car, he opened the door for Cherry. She jumped in without hesitation. She already knew the drill when it came to their trips. He rolled down the window so that she could stick her head out and enjoy the wind.

The route to the countryside was one of Krassy's favorites. Winding roads took them up into the mountains.

Rolling hills dotted the countryside. It was a nice time of year, with plenty of wildflowers and colors popping in the green grass.

"Look at those fields! They'd be perfect for you to run in, wouldn't they?"

Krassy pulled the car up to the parking lot for the natural trails where they would be spending the day. In the distance, tall trees stood like guardians against the horizon as white clouds drifted slowly across the sky.

"This looks like the perfect spot," Krassy said, finding a small clearing near a little stream that glistened in the sunlight. It was surrounded by tall grasses and a few scattered wildflowers.

He spread out the picnic blanket while Cherry took off down the hill to an open field. She rolled around in the grass, biting off the tops of flowers and leaping into the air. Krassy smiled at the sight.

"Here's a snack, Cherry," he called her back to the blanket after a while, holding something, his hand closed. She trotted over with curiosity, sniffing his fingers. "Here you go, girl," Krassy opened his hand, offering her a treat. She gulped it down without chewing.

"You know, Cherry," he said, biting into his sandwich, "we should do this more often."

Sometimes he found himself overoccupied with work or getting distracted with day-to-day things.

It was hard to find the time to take an entire day to spend with Cherry, but when he did, it helped him get away from the normal grind.

After they enjoyed their snack, Krassy took pictures of the rolling hills, the serene stream, and, of course, Cherry, who moved around, making it nearly impossible for Krassy to get a clear shot of her.

"Cherry, would you just hold still for a moment?" Krassy adjusted his camera. He wanted to get a few good shots of Cherry.

He was working on a photo wall, and Cherry was the center piece of that, since she was such a huge part of his life. Cherry had other plans.

She didn't care about pictures or capturing memories. Krassy kept thinking that she would run out of energy and then she'd be still, but of course, he was wrong.

When Cherry found a shallow stream with frogs hopping here and there, all hopes of a clear picture were washed down the drain. Cherry jumped from rock to rock, her attention zoned in on one particular frog that was leading her on.

Krassy watched as the frog zipped ahead, dodging here and there, barely avoiding Cherry. He could see that his dog, though, was capable of catching up. As she leapt to the last rock, he lifted his camera to get a shot mid-jump.

At the last moment, Cherry stepped wrong on the rock and fell over, splashing into the water below.

"You sure know how to make a mess." Krassy laughed heartily. Cherry stood and took up a funny stance, as if she was surprised by her fall.

"Oh wait, wait…" Krassy took a step back, but he wasn't fast enough. Cherry shook from head to toe, flinging bits of water and mud in every direction, including all over Krassy's clothes.

After drying off, Cherry and Krassy returned to the blanket and enjoyed the warm sun and gentle breeze.

Krassy took a few more photos, finally capturing a lovely portrait of Cherry sitting proudly, her tongue lolling out and her fur sparkling in the sun.

It didn't take long for both Krassy and Cherry to recover their energy, and another walk was on the schedule.

They took off across one of the bigger fields, with Cherry leading the way. She stopped to investigate every rock on the side of the road and stuffed her nose into every clump of flowers.

Krassy didn't mind the detours. He found he rather enjoyed getting detailed pictures of the flowers and the surroundings.

"What are you trying to find?" Krassy asked when he spotted Cherry digging furiously.

To his astonishment, a tin box, covered in rust, sat at the bottom of the hole that Cherry had just finished digging.

"Wow. What do we have here?" He pushed off the rest of the dirt and pulled the little box up to ground level. He undid the rusty latch and flipped open the lid.

There, inside, were a handful of old coins and a faded image. He couldn't tell if they were valuable or just something left behind, but either way, it was a cool find.

"How nice, you've managed to dig up a little chunk of history," Krassy said.

Cherry looked very proud of herself.

Happy and a bit tired, they made their way back to the car after a day of adventure.

Back at home, Krassy cleaned the old coins and framed the photograph. He placed them on a shelf as a tribute to their day in the country, which he wouldn't be forgetting anytime soon. He had no idea of the worth of the coins, as they looked pretty old, but to him, they were a special reminder of his day out in the country with Cherry.

Camping

Camping was something Krassy wanted to do with Cherry for quite a while. When the weekend he'd circled on the calendar approached, he anticipated the outing with eagerness. He started putting everything in the car, and Cherry instantly stuck underfoot, an anxious air about her.

"I'm not going anywhere without you," Krassy ruffled her fur reassuringly as he set their tent in the back of his car.

Cherry's tail wagged so hard that it looked like it might fall off. She loved the outdoors, which made him certain she was going to enjoy camping. Her eyes sparkled with excitement, reflecting the sunset.

Krassy finished with the packing, then continued on with their evening routine. They would leave early the next morning.

It was still dark in the morning, when he got Cherry, and they set out toward a remote mountain area where he'd picked up a wild camping spot on the map. Cherry rested her head out the window, her ears flapping in the wind, and Krassy sang along to his favorite songs.

It was two hours away to the destination, and as they pulled up, the sun was just rising over the mountain, casting golden trails through the pine branches.

They left the car in a small parking lot to the side of the road, and they continued on foot for about half an hour before reaching the place. Krassy started to unload everything from his big backpack while Cherry wandered off to explore the bubbling stream nearby.

When Cherry came back from making her first impression of the place, he called her over.

"Hey, girl, help me set up camp," Krassy said, patting the rucksack.

As he unloaded, Cherry helped him, dragging different things to the middle of the site and inspecting everything as he made a pile on the ground. Cherry found the whole process fascinating and tried to assist by carrying the stakes around in her mouth; her energy was impressive.

After the camp was set up, it was time for a hike. Krassy took his bottle of water and a few snacks in a small bag, and they set off on one of the forest trails.

Cherry led the way with her nose to the ground, discovering all sorts of scents. She found every squirrel worthy of a chase. Cherry jumped over logs, avoided puddles, and scuffled through the leaves.

When they found a little clearing with a pond in the center of it, Krassy had a feeling it would be Cherry's favorite spot on their walk. The water was clear and inviting, reflecting the leafy canopy above.

"Are you up for a quick swim, Cherry?" Krassy asked.

She didn't need any convincing. Cherry jumped into the water, splashing around and barking with joy. Krassy sat on a nearby rock, watching her have a wonderful time.

Cherry took forever to swim. She went back and forth, jumping in and out.

Her natural love of water made it look as if she was equally comfortable with water or land.

After some time of enjoying the pond, she came out one last time, shaking right beside Krassy and sending a spray of water in his direction. He didn't mind the refreshing droplets.

"Let's move on, Cherry," Krassy stood up and she followed him. They left the clearing and the pond and continued on the hiking trail. A good half hour later, they found a wide meadow, full of wildflowers.

Krassy sat down on the soft grass, and Cherry flopped down next to him, panting happily. Krassy enjoyed some sandwiches he'd brought along and tossed Cherry her favorite snacks, which she gladly devoured.

A yellow butterfly playfully flew over Cherry's nose as if taunting her. She tilted her head from side to side, watching it curiously. Once or twice, she tried to catch it, but without success. Krassy couldn't stop laughing as Cherry chased the butterfly with endless energy.

This went on for some time before Cherry got bored and a little tired. She dropped out of the chase, and the butterfly disappeared in the air.

"Time to head back to the campsite, Cherry," Krassy looked at the setting sun. The shadows grew longer, and the air became cooler.

Night noises popped up as the evening came in.

A spooky howl of a coyote somewhere in the distance echoed through the woods, sending shivers down Krassy's spine.

When they got to camp, Krassy built a campfire. Flames crackled warmly, sending up sparks dancing in the dark. Cherry sat by the fire and next to Krassy, both with a content look on their faces.

After dinner, the stars began to twinkle overhead like a thousand tiny diamonds.

The noises in the woods took a bit to get used to, but after a while, Krassy found them comforting in a way. He told Cherry stories about the constellations, pointing out shapes in the night sky.

Cherry listened with her head resting peacefully on Krassy's lap. Her eyes half-closed, lulled by the soothing rhythm of his voice.

They were just about to call it a night when Cherry's ears perked up as small antennas as if she heard something. She stood up, her nose twitching as she caught an unfamiliar scent.

There, in the shadows of the fire, a whole family of deer walked cautiously from the woods. Their eyes reflected the firelight as they nibbled on the grass.

They were cautious and yet brave as they enjoyed their late evening meal, not minding Krassy and Cherry's presence.

After a few moments, the deer family disappeared back in the shadows of the trees.

The night became cooler and darker. Krassy and Cherry crawled into the tent. The fabric rustled softly as Cherry snuggled up close to Krassy, her warmth comforting in the cold night air.

"Goodnight, Cherry. Thank you for coming camping with me," Krassy said.

Cherry's tail thumped softly against the sleeping bag in response, like the sound of a heartbeat.

Then they fell asleep under a blanket of a billion stars, dreaming of their next adventures, with the forest standing guard around them, a silent witness to their bond and the magic of their shared journey.

Too Close

It was a sunny day at the park—a place Krassy and Cherry visited often. Her favorite toy was the flying disk now; she loved it more every time they played with it. Krassy had purchased another one so that she'd have a couple different colors. He swore she'd choose a different one depending on the day.

Cherry's tongue hung from her mouth from her efforts to catch the disk. The weather was beautiful, making the afternoon almost surreal.

Krassy lifted his wrist and threw the disk harder than ever. It soared higher than it had all afternoon, and Cherry took off after it. She leapt up into the air like she had all the other times. Only this time, she hadn't noticed the sharp branch on the ground.

Krassy's eyes found the danger just as Cherry came crashing down, the disk in her mouth and a triumphant look in her eye. One second later, she yelled in pain as she crashed to the ground, her leg falling against the log and the sharp stick jutting out.

Her yelps filled the air.

"Cherry!" Krassy shouted, panic rising in his chest. She stood up, limping toward him. He rushed over to her, his mind racing. He bent down to examine the wound. Blood seeped from a large cut on her leg, staining the grass red. Without a moment's hesitation, Krassy grabbed her up in his arms and ran towards the car. They had to get to the vet.

Fortunately, the clinic wasn't far away. The sight of the small, white building helped ease a little of the anxiety in Krassy's chest. The vet rushed the injured dog to the examination room.

"Cherry was very lucky," the doctor said to Krassy after a quick assessment. "The wound is really close to one of her main arteries. If this artery had been damaged in any way, she couldn't have made it to our clinic. She was dangerously close to a tragic incident. Please have a seat in the waiting room over there. I'll need a few more minutes to take care of her."

"Alright, and thank you so much!" Krassy took a seat and waited impatiently in the clean and brightly illuminated lobby area. The unique and distinct antiseptic scent filled the air.

The minutes seemed like hours for Krassy, thoughts racing in his mind about the unlucky accident when he heard a door opening.

"I've stitched her up well," the vet finally came out the emergency room. "Don't you worry, she's strong. She'll be okay," he said with a comforting smile. "She simply needs a few weeks of good rest so her leg heals completely."

Each week, Krassy brought Cherry to the clinic for regular check-ups to ensure her recovery was going well.

Cherry's leg healed completely after several weeks, and she was back to her usual, energetic self.

To celebrate, Krassy decided to play with Cherry on the grassy field in front of their home.

This time, they used a tennis ball instead of the flying disk. It was a peaceful evening, and the air smelled like freshly cut grass from that afternoon when he'd trimmed the yard.

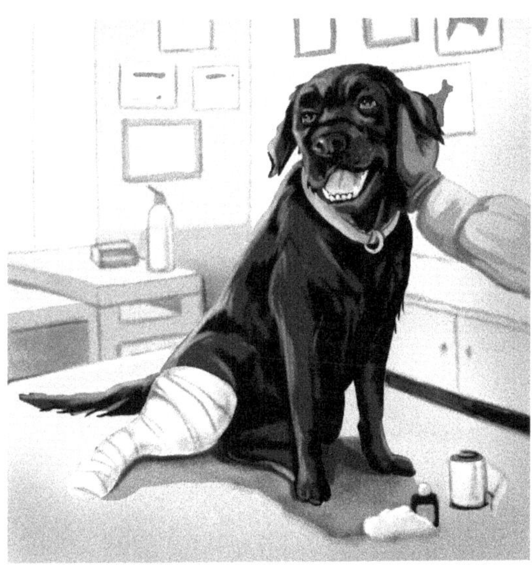

Krassy tossed the ball, and Cherry dashed after it. She was almost back to her old self, and that set Krassy at ease after being so close to losing her.

Cherry snapped at the ball, her teeth brushing against it and sending it into the street. Cherry barked as she chased after the bouncing ball without looking around.

A car was driving down the road. It turned the corner, barreling down the street.

"Cherry, stop!" Krassy shouted. Desperation coursed through him. She was too focused on the ball to pay attention. The car screeched to a stop as the driver tried to avoid Cherry. She disappeared under the car.

Krassy paled at the sight. His body froze in fear before he rushed forward, terrified of what was waiting for him.

Cherry appeared from under the car, completely unscathed, with the tennis ball in her mouth. It was a miracle.

The driver's body sagged with relief when he saw her, tail wagging and all.

"Thank God she's okay. Is she hurt?" He asked.

"She seems fine. I think you stopped in the nick of time." Krassy rushed to Cherry, tears of relief flowing down his face.

He pulled her close and looked for any signs of injury, but there were none.

He carefully touched her body and ruffled her fur to make sure Cherry was not in pain. It all looked okay.

"I didn't see her until the very last second, just before she vanished." The driver ran a hand through his hair. "I'm so sorry."

"It's not your fault," Krassy replied, his voice shaky. "She chased the ball into the street. I'm just glad she's alright."

The driver leaned down and gently patted Cherry's back.

"You're a lucky girl," he said softly. Cherry responded by wagging her tail even more, most likely unaware of her second near scrape with disaster.

Krassy let out a long breath of relief. "I need to be more careful. She means the world to me."

"I'm really glad she's okay." The driver said, shaking his head with disbelief still on his face.

"I should probably go." He said goodbye to Krassy and Cherry with more apologies before disappearing into his car and driving down the street.

"You almost gave me a heart attack." Krassy wrapped his arms tightly around Cherry's neck, his voice shaking with emotion.

Cherry licked his face, unfazed by the whole ordeal. She grabbed the tennis ball with her mouth and showed it to Krassy with a look of pride in her eyes as if to say, "I found it."

Cherry had managed to survive two narrow misses on losing her life. Krassy was going to have to be a little more careful. These incidents reminded him of how fragile a dog could be and how a simple error could steal her away in the blink of an eye.

After the situation with the car, Krassy put up a fence around his yard the next day.

He made sure that whenever they played together, things were as safe as possible.

They played inside the new fence, and when they went to the park, he'd check the ground for anything that could be dangerous.

It was always on the forefront of his mind how close he'd come to losing Cherry. If Krassy had learned one thing besides safety and how much she loved her tennis ball, it was that Cherry was more than just a dog; she was his loyal companion and his best friend.

Snow

Krassy stood by the window in his bedroom. A fresh blanket of white snow covered everything. It was one of the rare mornings where he was up before Cherry. She was still curled up in her bed on the floor, her nose tucked under her paw.

"Cherry," he whispered, shaking her softly. "Wake up! It snowed!" Cherry's ears perked up, then her eyes popped open. "Come see," he called her over.

She dashed to the window, and her breath fogged up the glass as she stared at the wonderland. She had the most satisfying reaction of wondering that made Krassy laugh. What would she do once they went outside?

Krassy bundled up in the warmest clothes he could, pulling on a thick, woolen scarf and gloves.

"Ready to go out, girl?" He asked, grabbing her leash. Cherry barked in return, her tail wagging so hard it almost knocked over a lamp.

It was freezing outside, the air a crisp, brittle temperature. The world was quiet; all of the normal, busy sounds were muffled by the powdery snow. It was almost blinding to look at. The white surface glittered with reflections from the sun.

Cherry started with a couple of cautious steps before she took a leaping jump. After all, it was frozen water if Krassy considered it logically. Krassy laughed as he watched her play, her black fur frosted with the bright white snow.

"Let's go to the park, Cherry," Krassy said. "I bet it's beautiful there with all this snow." Cherry barked in agreement and led the way, her nose twitching as she sniffed the icy air. The park was breathtaking. It was the picture of winter. The empty branches of the park were covered in snow, heavy under the weight.

Cherry wasted no time. She was new to the snow but not new to having fun. She started rolling in a patch of snow, as if she was making a dog-shaped snow angel. Krassy joined in on the fun with a chuckle. He got down beside her to make a real snow angel.

Their breath made puffs of fog in the chilly air. Side by side, they continued with their angels. When Cherry was done with hers, she stood and got closer to Krassy, covering his face in wet, slobbery kisses.

"How about a snowball chase, Cherry?" Krassy said, standing up and scooping up a handful of snow and making a ball out of it. He threw it at Cherry. Powdery snow fell all over her as it connected.

She barked, trying to catch the snowball in mid-air. Krassy made another snowball, tossing it a bit farther this time. Cherry chased after it, pouncing on the snow and barking joyfully.

She bit into the ball, disintegrating it into a puff of ice. The snowball fight had them wearing their energy out a bit, so Krassy decided it was time for another time-honored snow tradition.

The snowman.

"I think you're going to love what we're doing next, Cherry." He picked a spot that had plenty of snow.

It didn't take long to finish shaping three big snowballs, then it was time for assembly. It was harder than he remembered, but eventually he managed to stack the three balls up into a lopsided, leaning snowman.

Some black stones were perfect for the eyes, and Cherry dropped a piece of orange plastic she found under a park bench at his feet.

"Thank you, Cherry; this is great for the nose."

He pulled his scarf off and wrapped it around the snowman's neck before he asked Cherry to sit in front of it, then leaned in and used the camera he'd stuffed into his pocket to snap a picture. Their first snow together was a memory he wanted to save.

Cherry barked, looking pleased with her efforts to help. Krassy was pretty happy with their creation himself.

They stood there, admiring the snowman from afar, when half a dozen kids walked nearby.

Krassy recognized some of his neighbors' kids and waved to them.

"Hey!" they waved back. One of them held up his sled. "Does Cherry want to try sledding?"

"I think she'd love that." Krassy followed the kids, leading Cherry along with him. He hadn't been sledding in forever, so in a way it was a first they'd share together.

The kid he spoke to handed him a large black sled. "Why don't the two of you go before us?"

"Thanks." Krassy positioned the sled at the top of the hill and patted the front for Cherry to join him. She didn't hesitate at all, highlighting her overly trusting personality.

He wrapped one arm around her, and with the other, he held onto the rope lead for the sled.

They scooted forward, and the next thing Krassy knew, they were shooting down the hill. It was exhausting. For the rest of the afternoon, they went up and down the hill, enjoying ride after ride. After sledding, there were snow forts to be built and a bigger snowball fight with all the kids. Cherry was the star of the day. All of the kids loved having her there.

By late afternoon, it was time to head back to the house for something to eat and to get warm.

They said goodbye to their friends and hurried home. Krassy started a fire in the fireplace after they'd eaten and sat down with his hot cocoa. Cherry couldn't have the delicious drink as it was too warm for her, so he made sure she had one of her favorite treats to enjoy instead.

They sat there together as the sun began to set. Krassy ran a hand over Cherry's black fur, which glowed in the soft firelight.

"You know, Cherry, today was one of the best days ever," Krassy said, looking down at her. "You made it a lot of fun."

Cherry looked up at Krassy with her big, brown eyes and gave his hand a gentle lick. The fire crackled, filling the living room with a cozy atmosphere.

As the sun sank lower outside, snowflakes began to fall again, covering the snow they'd enjoyed so much with another blanket for a fresh coat the next day. Krassy knew that having Cherry by his side would make even the coldest winter day be full of warmth and friendship.

Waiting for the Train

Krassy and Cherry stood at the city train station, waiting for a friend. It was a crowded place, full of people rushing, coming, and going. Cars lined the street outside, waiting to pick up loved ones, friends, and passengers.

Krassy's hand tightened on Cherry's leash. She was a nervous ball of energy, tantalized by the different scents and activities. The air was full of noises, the sounds of rumbling engines and distant trains clattering on the tracks.

Krassy and Cherry wandered about in the train station for a while before they went back outside. He was trying to avoid the normal disasters that often happened when she got loose. Near the station entrance, Cherry's nose caught an intriguing scent.

Her nose sniffed at the air, and she pulled Krassy towards the source of the smell.

"Where are you going, Cherry?" He followed her down the sidewalk, wondering where she was so determined to go.

She had a mind of her own and had no problems showing Krassy what she wanted by dragging him along. Cherry led Krassy to a silver sedan with its passenger-side window rolled down. A young man sat inside the car, reading a book. Next to him was a paper bag of dog treats. It was open, and Cherry could most likely smell them. The man peered out at the two of them, a smile spreading across his face.

"Hey there," the man said. He grabbed a treat from the bag and held it up, looking to Krassy for confirmation. Krassy nodded; it would probably be fine for him to give it to Cherry. The man tossed the treat to the dog through the open window. Cherry gulped the treat down, licking her lips as if asking for more. Krassy stepped a little closer with a smile.

"I'm Zachary," The man had black hair and brownish eyes.

"I'm Krassy, and this is Cherry." Krassy finished the introduction. "It looks like you made a new friend."

The man chuckled. "I'm waiting for someone to arrive with a dog, so I got these treats. It seems your dog likes them too, and there are plenty. She can have a few more if you don't mind." He handed Cherry another cookie, and she accepted it again.

"Thanks for the dog treats. Cherry will accept anything she can eat." They both laughed. Cherry's appetite was something only a fellow dog person would understand.

A rumble came from the sky, and a moment later, a light drizzle began to fall, making a thrumming patter on the pavement.

"Why don't you come in the car to shelter from the rain?" Zachary said to Krassy. "There's lots of space in the car."

Just as Krassy was about to politely decline, and before he could do anything to stop her, Cherry leaped through the open window and landed on the passenger seat as if she understood the invitation was for her.

Zachary threw his head back with a hearty laugh. Cherry wagged her tail proudly, very pleased with herself. Krassy shook his head with disbelief and a little chuckle.

"Cherry, come back here," he scolded. "I am so sorry for what just happened."

"Don't worry. It's fine." Zachary replied. "It seems that Cherry just took me up on my invitation. Did you know some say Labradors are as smart as a four-year-old kid?

They can't talk, but if you look carefully, they give you all sorts of signs; they know what's going on around them." His gaze glowed with interest as he continued on.

"They can solve problems on their own and learn things from the environment—things like figuring out how to open doors and child-proof locks, getting food, and communicating with humans."

He gave Cherry an admiring look. "Actually, Labradors can read human emotions and body language. They can detect sadness, happiness, anxiety, or fear and adapt their behavior accordingly."

It seemed Zachary knew a lot about Labradors.

Krassy nodded.

"I've noticed that about Cherry. She is very smart. I'm sure she understands many words, and what just happened serves as confirmation.

A distant sound of the train whistle filled the air. The train had arrived.

"Looks like my friend is here." Zachary peered down the sidewalk.

"Thanks again for the treats." Krassy said, opening the door for Cherry. Cherry jumped out, wagging her tail, clearly pleased with the unexpected adventure.

"Ready to go, Cherry?" Krassy asked. Cherry barked in response, as if saying goodbye to their new friend. Zachary waved goodbye, and Krassy waved back.

"You really are something else, Cherry." Krassy said as they walked back into the train station. "Always full of surprises. It's amazing how you can understand so many things."

Cherry looked up at him, her eyes bright and full of understanding. She might not have known every word, but she could sense that he'd said something sweet and kind.

After they picked up their friend, Krassy told him all about their little run-in with Zachary and how Cherry made herself at home in a stranger's car for some dog treats. Krassy's friend found it funny and gave it a good laugh.

The three of them walked home together, going over the story in detail and discussing everything Krassy learned about Labradors from Zachary. He thought that he was only scratching the surface of what he would learn on their upcoming adventures. Krassy had a feeling there were many more just around the corner—his feeling would soon turn a reality.

Traces, we left so many in the snow—
traces, cleaner than a teardrop.

Reminder of the laughter and bark in the wild,
moments of joy, pure like a small child.
The snow will melt, but more will fall,
to cover the warm memories, preserving them all.
Deep, they'll stay for eternity's call.

Thanks for the adventures and the smiles, Cherry!
…and for the unforgettable memories!

Final words

I want to express my heartfelt gratitude to my family for their unwavering support throughout my journey. Their encouragement, love, and understanding have been an ongoing source of strength and inspiration for me.

I am forever thankful for my best friend, the Labrador Cherry, who has filled my days with endless joy and lots of smiles through our adventures over the years. Her unconditional love and loyalty have enriched my life in ways I could have never imagined…

About the author

I'm a passionate explorer who has spent countless hours in remote outdoors with my black Labrador dog, Cherry, and our friends. These experiences have shaped my deep appreciation for the natural world and the friendships forged through shared adventures, finding happiness in the joy and wonder of the simplest moments of life, whether in the busy city or in the tranquil wilderness.

Scan the QR code or visit https://bit.ly/m/krasimir

Send me an email:
krasi.mir@yahoo.com

Visit my Facebook profile:
www.facebook.com/krasi.mir.author

Join my reader's group:
www.facebook.com/groups/krasi.mir.readers

www.ingramcontent.com/pod-product-compliance
Lightning Source LLC
Chambersburg PA
CBHW061143160726
48006CB00038B/2175